T0381373

Naila, and the Magical Forest

Shanon Stovell

Thank you to all of my loved ones that have helped me along the way and I am so grateful for the many lessons acquired.

To order additional copies of this book, contact:
Xlibris
1-888-795-4274
www.Xlibris.com
Orders@Xlibris.com

ISBN: Softcover   978-1-4535-1385-9
         EBook   978-1-9845-8788-6

Print information available on the last page

Rev. date: 07/02/2020

On the first day of spring the sun was shining, birds were chirping and the cool breeze rustled the leaves ever so gently. It was the most beautiful day this year.

The warmth of the air made Naila feel all tingly inside. She was so excited to be going outside for she had been ill all of the previous week from a terrible cold. Today Naila wore her favorite outfit with the most magnificent scarf she owned. Her father bought it for her on one of his many travels.

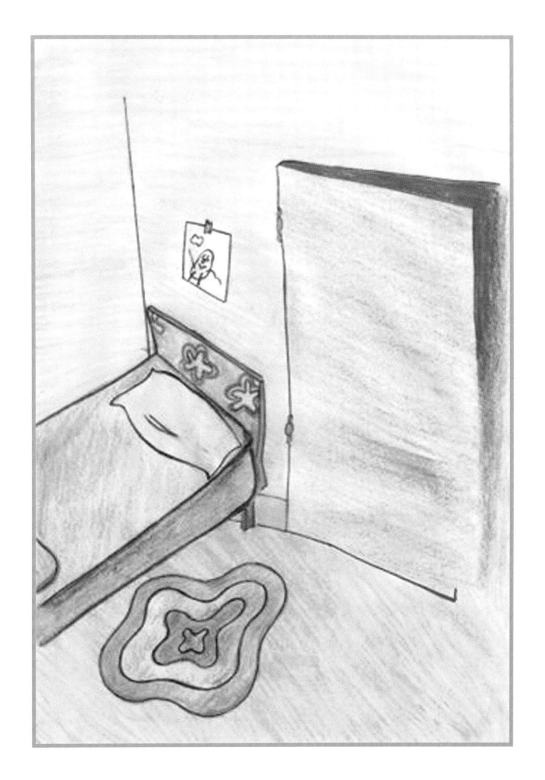

"Where are you and Penny planning on going today?" Her mother asked.
"Remember, you're not allowed to play in the forest behind Penny's house. It's too big and you could get hurt."

"I know mom." Naila said . . . . but she had already made up her mind that today would be a wonderful day to go exploring with Penny, even though their parents always forbade it.

Naila and Penny had been friends for a long time and did everything together. They loved going to play behind Penny's house. There were so many things to experience there.

They had built a fort when they were younger in the old funny looking tree that was in the very middle of the thicket. They visited this special place often, but didn't dare tell anyone.

Naila arrived at Penny's around noon. "Hurry up Penny! We have to go." She exclaimed.

As they started walking through the first set of trees, Naila tripped on an unusual stone in the middle of the path that made her fall pretty hard.

She was confused when she finished gathering herself for Penny was no where to be found. A piece of Penny's dress was hanging on a tree limb near by. Things around her looked totally different now. "Penny!" She yelled. Penny didn't answer. "Where am I?" Naila thought to herself. "Mother always told us that this isn't a place to play."

The sky was still bright and beautiful. Naila was very nervous now but convinced herself that she would be ok. The trees and bushes around her were now glistening in the sunlight. As she looked closer at the leaves she discovered they were of bright and shimmering colors.

She reached up and picked a few of the leaves off of the tree closest to her. Then she heard a peculiar sound. It was a soft whimper. She paid the noise no mind until she discovered where it was coming from.

Naila stopped and listened closely and realized that it was the tree that was crying. She had never heard of trees crying before. She felt terrible so whispered a sincere apology and placed the leaves that she had picked onto the ground near the base of the tree's trunk.

While looking down she saw one of Penny's shoes. She was quickly amazed to
see that the pebble path was no longer pebbles at all. They were jewels. Rubies,
diamonds, emeralds . . . she placed as many as she could into her pockets.
"I need to find Penny." She thought.

Just then she heard voices coming from above. "Hello! Who's there?"

The voices stopped for a moment. Naila looked up and saw two squirrels.

"Is she looking at us?" Mr. Squirrel said aloud. "I don't know." Mrs. Squirrel responded.

Naila's eyes grew with amazement when she realized the voices that she was hearing were coming from the squirrels' mouths.

"You can talk?" She asked.

"Of course we can. All of the animals here can." Mrs. Squirrel answered.

"Can you please help me? My friend and I were split up and I think something has happened to her. I need to find her."

"No I'm sorry we can't help you. We are much too busy. The winter will be here before we know it and we need to collect food. It was nice meeting you though. Goodbye!"

The two squirrels scurried away and left Naila standing there all alone. It was getting dark and now she was scared, hungry, and wanted to go home. She desperately needed to find her friend. "I should have listed to my mother."

"What am I going to do now?"

"Follow me!" A deep rumbling voice bellowed.

Right in front of her there stood a giant troll with a crooked smile and jagged yellowish teeth. He held a large spear in his right hand and had on a tattered brown shirt. The sight of him frightened her so much that she couldn't think of doing anything else but run. So she did.

She ran and ran until she couldn't run anymore. When she stopped to take a breath, she looked around and noticed that she had run right into what seemed to be the village of trolls. Their houses were everywhere. Big ones, small ones, odd ones, long ones. One of the younger trolls noticed Naila and yelled, "Intruder!" Everyone's attention was now on her.

Naila was about to run again when the giant troll she had encountered in the forest previously was standing in front of the door to a large bird cage almost at the center of the village next to a steamy boiling pot. The steam was so thick that it was hard to make out the figure that was sitting in the cage. The wind started to blow just enough for the steam to lighten. "Penny!" Naila screamed in horror as she finally realized that the figure in the cage was her friend.

"Naila? Get me out of here!"

Naila tricked the trolls by running out of the village and then back again. She hid behind one of the smaller houses closest to the pot.

Naila noticed that someone had dropped the keys on the ground next to the cage. When she saw that, she ran over and picked them up as fast as she could, unlocked the cage and pulled Penny to freedom. They ran out of that village so fast that it felt that they were running on air.

Never looking back, they ended up finding themselves in a dark forest. They were scared, hungry and tired. Eyes were watching them from everywhere.

"We need to find a way home." Penny said.

Tears began running down Naila's face. "Yes. Yes we do."

They decided to continue their journey homeward bound. Over a few hills and through a few valleys, they continued to go forward until they came to a small swamp.

"We need to cross this." Said Penny.

They were both so scared but knew that this was the best decision.

As they sloshed through the swamp, something brushed past their feet.

"What was that?" Naila squealed.

"I don't know."

"There it is again."

Looking down Naila saw a ferocious beast. It was a three headed crocodile with razor sharp teeth.

"Run!" She screamed.

Just then a handsome Prince leaped out of nowhere and wrestled the creature. He killed the beast with a jab, a punch, and a swift slice of his sward. The three headed monster was destroyed.

"Who are you?" Naila asked.

"I am Prince Isa. I heard your cries so I came to make sure you return home safely." He said. "Follow me. I will show you the way."

They proceeded into another part of the forest. The Prince led the girls into a beautiful cave behind a waterfall. There he told them that that would be the perfect place where they could all rest for the night. He made them a fire to keep them warm.

Morning came quickly. Prince Isa gathered breakfast for them. Soon after the three of them ate, they followed the brave Prince back into the forest, through the valleys and over the hills . . . It was around noon and Penny's house could be seen in the distance. The girls were so grateful to the Prince for finding the way home. Their journey was long and tiring. Penny thanked him and took off running towards her house. "I'll never forget you Isa."

"When will I *see* you again?" Naila asked.

"I have always watched over you. If you want to *see* me again, just call my name." He said.

"That's all?"

"That's all."

The next morning Naila woke up in her own bed to the wonderful aromas of her mother's cooking.

She brushed her teeth and rushed out to the dining room for breakfast.

Her mother and grandmother were there waiting to greet her with warm smiles. "We missed you last night. Did you have fun at Penny's house?" Naila realized that her mother would never believe her if she told her about the magical forest and all of the adventures they had had. She had finally learned her lesson and decided that she would never disobey her mother again. So she simply said, "Yes mom."

Naila and Penny's adventure was like a dream. Neither one of them could believe that those events had truly happened but neither one of them ever went into the forest alone again.

The girls always listened to their parents after that and everyone lived happily ever after.

The End.

Printed in the United States
By Bookmasters